When a DRAGON moves in

Written by Jodi Moore   Illustrated by Howard McWilliam

Flash
Light
PRESS

TO LARRY, ALEX & STEVE, MY MUSES, MY LOVES –JM   FOR REBECCA –HM

If you build a perfect sandcastle,
a dragon will move in.

He'll settle in all cozy
and peep at you from inside...

...and you'll wonder how you ever got so lucky.

With a dragon in your castle, you'll have a built-in marshmallow toaster,

your very own raft,

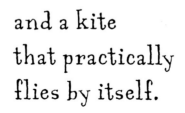

and a kite
that practically
flies by itself.

Best of all, no beach bully would dare
stomp your castle with a dragon inside.

Of course, there are rules on the beach,
so you'll have to hide his smoke
from the lifeguard...

ON
DUTY

...and erase the dragon prints from the sand.

Eventually, you'll want to share the great news with your family:

"There's a dragon in my castle," you'll call to your mom.

"Mmmm...hmmm," she'll answer.

"Listen to
him roar!"
you'll say.

"I hear the roar
of the ocean,"
she'll reply.

"See this feather from my dragon's wing?" you'll ask your dad.

"That's a nice seagull feather," he'll say,

"and you know what feathers are good for...."

"Feel my dragon's sharp teeth!" you'll shout.

"Those are just broken shells," your big sister will say.

But you and your dragon will know better.

Just about then, your dragon
will demand to be fed.

First he'll eat all of the peanut butter sandwiches...

...even the ones that were supposed to be for your sister.

Then his fiery snout
will make
the lemonade
sizzle.

"Stop blowing bubbles
in your drink,"
your mom will say.

"That wasn't me,"
you'll answer.
"That was the dragon."

And you'll hear a *heh-heh-heh* from deep inside the sandcastle.

Finally, since dragons love dessert, he'll slink into the family cooler and nibble the brownies when no one is looking.

"Whose fingerprints
are in the brownies?"
your dad will ask.

"Not fingerprints," you'll try to explain. "Dragon prints."

"There's no such thing as a dragon," your sister will say.

Then your dragon will snicker again, *heh-heh-heh*...

...and spray sand all over her.

"Young man, I don't think this is funny," your mom will say.

"That wasn't me," you'll answer. "It was the dragon."

"I think we've had enough of this dragon business," your dad will say.

"I guess I've had enough of this dragon business too," you'll sigh.

Then you'll march over to your sandcastle
and order your dragon to leave
until he learns some manners.

And you will vow

never to build

a perfect sandcastle

again.

At least until tomorrow.